# AS WE

# SOLDIER

## FOR OUR

# LAND

Patti Dunne Hunzeker

Archway Publishing books may be ordered through booksellers or by contacting:

Archway Publishing
1663 Liberty Drive
Bloomington, IN 47403
www.archwaypublishing.com
844-669-3957

Because of the dynamic nature of the Internet, any web addresses or links contained in this book may have changed since publication and may no longer be valid. The views expressed in this work are solely those of the author and do not necessarily reflect the views of the publisher, and the publisher hereby disclaims any responsibility for them.

ISBN: 978-1-6657-2741-9 (sc)
ISBN: 978-1-6657-2742-6 (e)

Print information available on the last page.

Archway Publishing rev. date: 09/07/2022

This book is dedicated to my four children, Jen, Jess, Becky, and Maggie, and my wonderful husband, Ken, all whom were SOLDIERS FOR OUR LAND.

# AS WE
# SOLDIER
## FOR OUR
# LAND

# GETTING READY

My daddy is going so far away, what should I do or say
Will he have strangers all around will he have time to play?

He's packing all his uniforms and all his combat gear
He's also packing books and pictures, that he holds oh so dear

I want to know how life will be for daddy far away
Where will he sleep, what will he eat, what will he do each day?
I am confused I don't know why; I am a bit scared too.
Do I tell daddy how I feel and why I am so blue?

He's looking down and all around, time passes on the clock
With flips and snaps and clips and cracks each bag does zip and lock.
He looks at me and smiles and smiles and hugs me oh so tight
And tells me that he'll miss me so, and think of me each night.

And then we walk into our den and Dad points with his hand
To a foreign place upon the map where he will soldier for our land.
He tells me what his job will be and that he's so prepared
He talks about the people there and says, "Please don't be scared."

He says he wants me to have fun, to work, to study and
By doing this then I will too be a soldier for our land.
I thank my daddy for our talk and for letting me discuss
And I promise him that I'll be good and have fun for both of us.

He leans right over and kisses me with cuddly bear in hand
And says to hug the bear each day as we soldier for our land.
A big bus comes to get my dad and takes him on his way
I feel so sad to see him go as I watch him drive away.

With bear in hand we head for home and now I start to wait
For the best day when my dad returns; I know it will be great!!!

# TIME AWAY

Daddy's now gone and I try so hard to play everyday and have fun
But sometimes I get so sad and mad until the day is done.
Then I remember that time will pass and soon he will be here
And I recall the words he said and I squeeze my teddy so dear.

Instead of yelling or being mean to all who come my way
I'll choose to draw a picture to share and mail to my daddy today.
I'll create a design of what I've done at school or during lunch
I'll draw my family and teacher too, or my friends all in a bunch.

I have an envelope that dad prepared for a moment just like this
I place my picture deep inside and seal it with a kiss.
I draw or write in my journal each day and then when my daddy comes home
I can share all I did while he was gone so he won't feel confused and alone.

I don't hear very much from my daddy each day and I do get very blue
So, I'll talk about this and continue to wait and I"ll cry a little bit, too
As each day goes by, I'll be kind and stay strong, and do as we both had planned
I'll follow the rules while I think of him as we both soldier for our land.

# COMING HOME

Dear Daddy you're coming home so soon it is only weeks away.
I need to tell you what I hope will happen on that day?
I hope you run right up to me and hug me with all your might
I hope you swing me all around and hold me oh so tight.

I hope that we can talk and share; I'll catch you up to date
I know you'll be so very tired but I hope we stay up late.
I hope you tell me all about your days so far away
I hope that you will have some stories and pictures of every day.

I hope in the mornings that we cook and that we can just kick back
I hope we can stay in our pajamas while I help you to unpack.
I heard that you have to work each day for a few hours or more
I hope each day when you return we can play just like before.

I heard that you might just have to sleep and rest your mind, it's true.
If that is a fact just tell me and I'll rest my mind with you.
I heard you saw many things so unkind and your heart must also rest too
If that is true just tell me and I'll rest my heart with you.

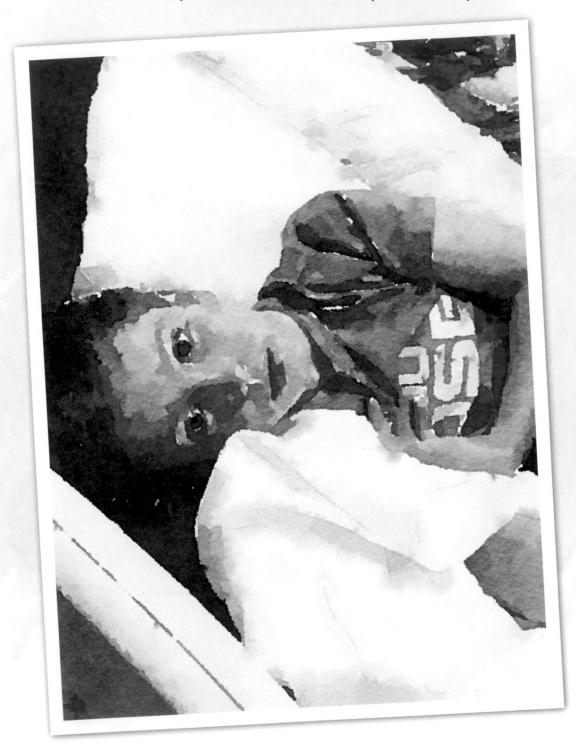

I hope you can talk to me and tell me all you learned and saw
You were away so long, I want to hear because I am in such awe.
I hope that you know that no matter what, I will always understand
You are my daddy and this I know we are both SOLDIERS FOR OUR LAND.

Printed in the United States
by Baker & Taylor Publisher Services